Paul Seller
Alphabats

Cuckoo Car
Adventure

TRANSWORLD PUBLISHERS LTD

LONDON • NEW YORK • TORONTO • SYDNEY • AUCKLAND

Big 'C' and Little 'c' live in a cottage down a crooked country lane.

It has a crooked door and windows with criss-cross panes.

There are colourful curtains and carpets, cushions on every chair, cupboards full of china cups and clocks... EVERYWHERE!

Clocks on tables,
clocks on floors,
tall clocks, small clocks,
clocks on drawers.

Clocks in corners,
clocks by chairs,
hall clocks, wall clocks,
clocks upstairs.

Suddenly, they all started to
chime at the same time!

BING! BANG! BONG!
CLING! CLANG! CLONG!
DING! DANG! DONG!

The Alphabats counted the chimes.

"Twelve o'clock!" said Little 'c'.
"What shall we do for lunch?"

"It's such a nice day," said Big 'C'.
"Let's take a picnic and go for
a ride in our car!"

The Alphabats raced to the kitchen and put a large cardboard box on the counter.

Then they packed it with their favourite picnic things.

Chicken sandwiches, potato crisps, cheese and crackers, cans of cold cola, cream cakes, custard pies and a big bag of chocolate chip cookies!

Little 'c' helped Big 'C' carry the box outside.

They went through the crooked door, along a concrete path, to the back of the cottage, where something special was concealed under a canvas cover.

A curious cow watched as the Alphabats carefully pulled off the cover and revealed...

A CLOCKWORK CAR!

Big 'C' and Little 'c' were SO clever. They had built their OWN car!

It was made of old clock cases and the wheels were gold clock faces.

The engine was a collection of cogs, chains, coils and rings. At the back was a big copper key to wind up the springs.

The Alphabats put the picnic box in the car. Then Big 'C' climbed in and closed the door.

"Could you crank the engine for me?" asked Big 'C'.

"Of course!" answered Little 'c' cheerfully.

Little 'c' crouched down behind the car, chin against chest, cheeks puffed out, clinging on to the key with both hands, and counted...

"One... two... THREE!"

Then, with a colossal heave, Little 'c' turned the copper key.

TIC-TOC... TIC-TOC...
The engine started.

Little 'c' ran round, clambered
in and closed the door.

The Alphabats' car crawled along
the road, past fields of cabbages,
carrots and corn.

They saw a scarecrow and
a cat curled up in a cart.

Soon, the clockwork car reached
the crest of a hill.

TIC-A-TOC... TIC-A-TOC...

The car cruised down the hill,
going faster and faster.

"Be careful!" cried Little 'c'.
"Some chickens are crossing the road!"

Big 'C' pressed the horn. Two small
doors opened at the front of the car.
Out popped a clockwork bird who
chirped... "CUCKOO! CUCKOO!"

The chickens cackled and ran clear.

TICKETY-TOC... TICKETY-TOC...
They couldn't stop!

The cuckoo car went round a corner,
over the kerb and crashed through
a fence.

The Alphabats clung on as the car
raced, out of control, towards
a gigantic tent. The tent was
covered in coloured lights
which flashed...

CIRCUS!... CIRCUS!... CIRCUS!

Inside the tent, a crowd of people were watching the comical clowns and the clever acrobats in the circus ring.

Suddenly, the cuckoo car burst through the curtains, charged across the ring...

And collided with the tent pole in the centre!

The Alphabats catapulted out of the car. The picnic box exploded like a cannon, shooting the contents into the air!

The man on the flying trapeze flew through crackers and chunks of cheese!

One currant bun hit the clown and his colourful trousers fell down!

Big 'C' and Little 'c' dived for cover.

Custard pies flashed past their eyes, chicken and bread dropped on their heads and potato crisps scattered like confetti!

A can of cola cascaded over the mayor, soaking his coat and his vest.

His wife chuckled, then let out a cry when a cream cake landed... SPLODGE! on her chest!

Big 'C' and Little 'c' crept out from behind the car.

They were certain that everyone would be very cross with them for crashing into the circus.

But, to their surprise, the crowd stood on their chairs and clapped and cheered.

Then the mayor called out,
"Congratulations! You are the
funniest clowns we have ever seen!"

Everybody crowded round with their
cameras to take pictures of
the Alphabats and their crazy car.

Big 'C' and Little 'c' smiled
and the clockwork bird chirped...

CUCKOO! CUCKOO!

CUCKOO CAR ADVENTURE
0 552 529001

First published in Great Britain by Transworld Publishers Ltd, 1995

CONDITIONS OF SALE

Transworld Publishers Ltd,
61-63 Uxbridge Road, London W5 5SA
Published in Australia by Transworld Publishers (Australia) Pty Ltd
15-25 Helles Avenue, Moorebank, NSW 2170
and in New Zealand by Transworld Publishers (NZ) Ltd
3 William Pickering Drive, Albany, Auckland

Made and printed in Great Britain